SAVING SUNSHINE

written by
Saadia Faruqi

art by
Shazleen Khan

:01
First Second
NEW YORK

CHAPTER 1

2

4

5

6

8

THANKS FOR COMING OUT SO EARLY IN THE MORNING TO GET CLEO, AMY!

DON'T WORRY, ZARA, I LOVE PET-SITTING HER.

OH, I'M GOING TO MISS YOU SO MUCH, CLEO!

HERE'S HER SPECIAL FOOD AND SOME TREATS...

...AND DON'T FORGET, HER COAT NEEDS TO BE COMBED EVERY DAY!

ER...SURE?

LET'S GO ZARA!

I'M TIRED OF BOTH OF YOU!
SHE'S FAKING.
SHE'S NOT REALLY HURT.
SHE'S JUST TRYING TO GET ME IN TROUBLE!
NO I'M NOT!
YES YOU ARE!
ENOUGH!
YOU TWO LEAVE ME NO CHOICE.
HAND OVER YOUR PHONES RIGHT NOW.

CHAPTER 2

41

44

45

56

65

YOU KNOW, I'LL ACTUALLY BE OKAY WITHOUT MY PHONE IF IT MEANS YOU MISSING SOME STUPID SPACE THINGY.

I BET THEY'VE PUT THE PHONES IN THE HOTEL SAFE.

OUR ROOM HAS A SAFE? COOL.

NOW LET'S MAKE A LIST OF POSSIBLE CODES FOR THE SAFE. IT'S USUALLY A FOUR-DIGIT NUMBER, SO I'M GUESSING BIRTHDAY?

WHY SHOULD I HELP YOU WITH ANYTHING?

BECAUSE YOU NEED THAT NATURE APP OF YOURS.

I HEAR THEY HAVE DOLPHINS HERE, AND STINGRAYS AND WHO KNOWS WHAT ELSE.

SO?

CHAPTER 3

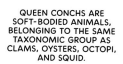
QUEEN CONCHS ARE SOFT-BODIED ANIMALS, BELONGING TO THE SAME TAXONOMIC GROUP AS CLAMS, OYSTERS, OCTOPI, AND SQUID.

AS AN EDIBLE MARINE SNAIL, THEY ARE IN DANGER OF EXTINCTION.

GOODBYE. BE SAFE!

?

WHAT THE...

95

I THINK I'M GOING TO TURN IN.

THE FIRST DAY OF CONFERENCE WAS BRUTAL.

ME TOO.

MORE FOOD FOR ME!

YOU GUYS GO AHEAD. I'LL BE THERE IN A MINUTE.

OH! THE YOUNG LADY FROM PAKISTAN! PARDON ME, I MEANT NEW YORK!

HOW CAN I HELP?

YEP, THAT'S ME!

IS THERE AN ANIMAL HOSPITAL NEARBY?

THE CLOSEST IS AN HOUR AND A HALF AWAY. WE'RE KIND OF IN A REMOTE LOCATION.

WHY?

THERE'S A BIG TURTLE ON THE BEACH. HE'S NOT MOVING AND I'M WORRIED ABOUT HIM.

CHAPTER 4

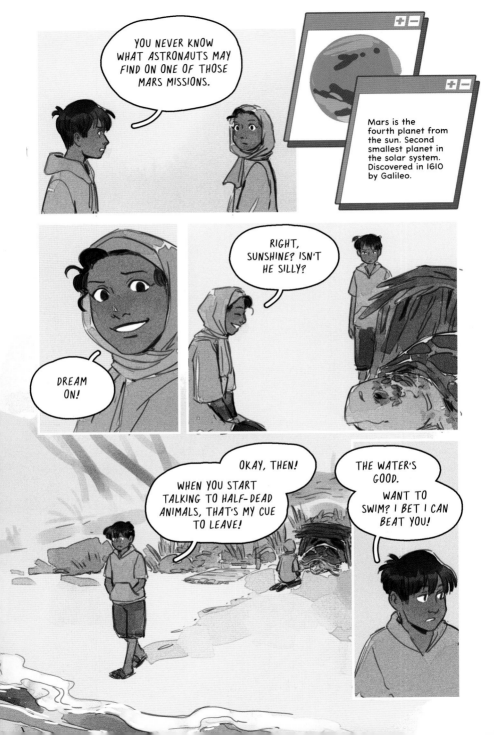

NO THANKS!

YOU LIKE MY SITTING HERE TALKING TO YOU, DON'T YOU, SUNSHINE?

I WISH I KNEW WHAT WAS WRONG WITH YOU.

I WISH I COULD HEAL YOU.

WHAT DOES ZARA KNOW? OF COURSE, OTHER PLANETS CAN HAVE LIFE.

WE JUST HAVEN'T DISCOVERED IT YET.

THIS IS MY LUCKY DAY!

YOU'RE RIGHT. IT'S NOT. IT'S A BIG DEAL—

ESPECIALLY FOR SOMEONE WHO JUST STARTED WEARING THE HIJAB A YEAR AGO.

I KNOW IT'S HARD, JAAN. BUT WE HAVE TO BE PATIENT AND KIND. HIJAB IS ALL ABOUT SACRIFICE.

NOT CARING WHAT OTHER PEOPLE THINK OF YOU.

IF YOU GET ANGRY AT EVERY PERSON WHO TAUNTS YOU, YOU'LL GET NOWHERE.

ALL THAT ANGER WILL JUST EAT YOU UP INSIDE. YOU HAVE TO LEARN TO IGNORE THEM.

I GUESS, YOU'RE RIGHT. HOW COME YOU'RE SO WISE, AMMA?

HA! IT COMES FROM YEARS OF EXPERIENCE.

WHAT DO YOU MEAN?

GROWING UP IN PAKISTAN, NOBODY CARED ABOUT MY HIJAB.

IT WAS PART OF THE CULTURE THERE...

...IN THE STREETS...

...IN MEDICAL SCHOOL...

...AT PARTIES.

BUT WHEN I CAME TO THE U.S.
EVERYTHING CHANGED.

I SUDDENLY BECAME THE ENEMY...

...AS A DOCTOR...

...AS A MOM.

THAT'S A LOGGERHEAD TURTLE. THE MOST COMMON SPECIES IN THE KEYS. THEY CAN LIVE UP TO...

...FIFTY YEARS. I KNOW.

GOOD JOB! YOU KNOW YOUR TURTLE FACTS.

YOU COULD SAY THAT.

CAN I ASK YOU SOMETHING?

GO RIGHT AHEAD!

WHERE DO THEY LIVE?

ARE THEY ALWAYS ALONE OR WITH THEIR MATES?

WHAT DO THEY EAT?

WHAT DO YOU DO IF THEY GET SICK?

SLOW DOWN! ONE QUESTION AT A TIME, PLEASE!

132

145

SUNSHINE! LOOK, I BROUGHT FOOD.

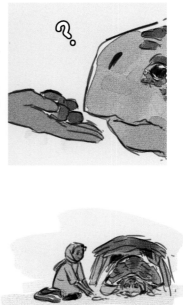

HOW HAVE YOU BEEN, MY JAAN?

YOUR JAAN? GIVE ME A BREAK!

THAT'S HORRIBLE!

WHAT ARE YOU TALKING ABOUT?

I GET IT NOW, ZARA.

ALL THAT ANIMAL RIGHTS STUFF. ALL YOUR OBSESSION...

I GET IT NOW!

WELL, I WOULDN'T CALL IT AN OBSESSION...

171

WHA...?

FORGET IT. I'M SO STUPID.

ZARA, WAIT!

FORGET HER, ZEESH. WANNA GO UP TO OUR ROOM AND PLAY VIDEO GAMES?

NO! YOU GUYS ARE AWFUL!

DON'T YOU KNOW YOU SHOULDN'T INSULT SOMEONE'S DRESS? WHAT SHE WEARS IS HER PERSONAL CHOICE.

CHAPTER 6

YES, SO WE CAN TAKE SOME PICTURES TO MARK YOUR AMAZING ACHIEVEMENT!

NICE TRY. BUT NO!

BUT WE'VE BEEN SO GOOD! WE'VE SPENT TIME TOGETHER WITHOUT FIGHTING.

RIGHT, ZARA?

I'M GLAD, BUT YOU HAVE TO FINISH YOUR PUNISHMENT. THAT'S THE ONLY WAY YOU'RE GOING TO LEARN.

YES! WE'VE GONE KAYAKING AND WALKED ON THE BEACH...

BUT... BUT...

THERE'S A LIVE EVENT FROM NASA STARTING ANY MINUTE NOW. IT'S A BIG DEAL!

HELP ME, ZEESH!

JUST ONE... MORE...PUSH...

:01

First Second

Published by First Second
First Second is an imprint of Roaring Brook Press,
a division of Holtzbrinck Publishing Holdings Limited Partnership
120 Broadway, New York, NY 10271
firstsecondbooks.com
mackids.com

Text © 2023 by Saadia Faruqi
Illustrations © 2023 by Shazleen Khan
All rights reserved

Library of Congress Control Number: 2022920570

Our books may be purchased in bulk for promotional, educational, or business use.
Please contact your local bookseller or the Macmillan Corporate and Premium Sales Department
at (800) 221-7945 ext. 5442 or by email at MacmillanSpecialMarkets@macmillan.com.

FIRST

EDITION

First edition, 2023
Edited by Samia Fakih
Cover design by Sunny Lee
Interior book design by Sunny Lee and Yan L. Moy
Production editing by Arik Hardin

Penciled on Procreate. Layout and bubble placement on Clip Studio.
Inked and colored on PaintTool SAI.

Printed in China by 1010 Printing International Limited,
Kwun Tong, Hong Kong

ISBN 978-1-250-79381-2 (paperback)
1 3 5 7 9 10 8 6 4 2

ISBN 978-1-250-79380-5 (hardcover)
1 3 5 7 9 10 8 6 4 2

Don't miss your next favorite book from First Second!
For the latest updates go to firstsecondnewsletter.com and sign up for our enewsletter.

BY ART
WE LIVE